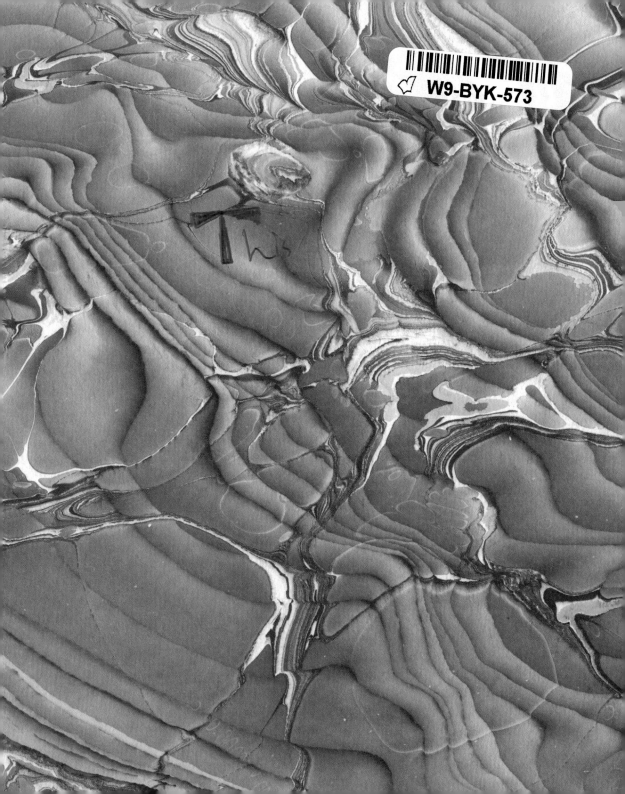

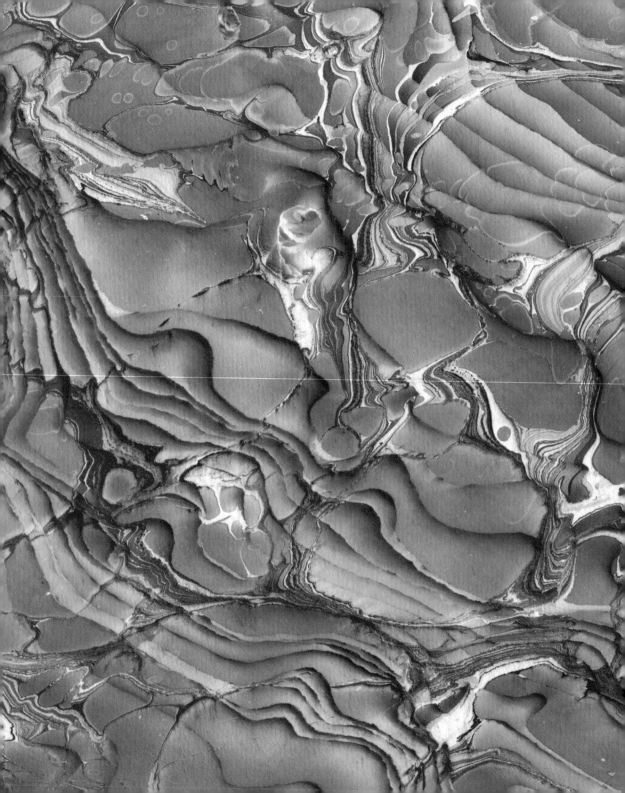

THE
Mythology
HANDBOOK

A COURSE IN ANCIENT GREEK MYTHS

BY LADY HESTIA EVANS

EDITED BY DUGALD A. STEER AND CLINT TWIST

London — New York — Athens

PRINTED FOR CANDLEWICK PRESS

PUBLISHERS OF RARE AND UNUSUAL BOOKS

Mythology™

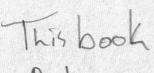

This book
Belong
to Rose
Rose

For Hector and Hippolyte,

from your affectionate mama

Text and design copyright © 2009 by The Templar Company Limited

The *Mythology* logo is a trademark of The Templar Company Limited

Illustrations copyright © 2009 by Nick Harris, James Kay,
Ian Miller, Nicki Palin, and David Wyatt

Narrative friezes by Helen Ward

Written by Dugald A. Steer and Clint Twist

Consultant: Olympia Bobou

First U.S. edition 2009

Library of Congress Cataloging-in-Publication Data is available.

Library of Congress Catalog Card Number 2008935650

ISBN 978-0-7636-4291-4

10 11 12 13 14 TLF 10 9 8 7 6 5

Printed in Dongguan, Guandong, China

CANDLEWICK PRESS

99 Dover Street
Somerville, Massachusetts 02144
www.candlewick.com
www.ologyworld.com

PUBLISHER'S NOTE

After the recent publication of a facsimile of John Oro's copy of *Mythology* by Lady Hestia Evans, we received this volume from a gentleman who claims to be a distant but direct descendant of that remarkable woman who made such a notable contribution to the study of the ancient Greek myths. The book, which was privately produced and has never before been published, was purportedly written by Lady Hestia for her two children, Hector and Hippolyte, as a means of introducing them to the wonders of Greek mythology while she was away unravelling ancient mysteries. We publish it here in the hope of doing the same for today's children. May the legends live on.

When travelling in Greece, it is advisable to adopt local styles of dress so as not to attract unwanted attention. Even Hector and Hippolyte might not recognise their dear mama were they to meet me in the guise of an Albanian merchant!

Lady Hestia Evans
IN ALBANIAN DISGUISE

A WARNING TO ALL MYTHOLOGISTS

THESE TALES OF GODS, HEROES, AND MEN are truly fascinating and are apt to take a powerful hold of one's imagination. However, the reader must be wary of placing too much belief in them. Some ancient Greek mysteries are best left unexplored, as demonstrated by the strange fate that seems to have befallen my unfortunate friend John Oro. Visitors to Greece are counselled to respect local customs at all times. In particular, they should refrain from trying to excavate ancient artefacts, which must always be left to the experts; the Greek authorities take a very dim view of amateur excavators. Furthermore, on no account should today's visitors be tempted to inscribe their names on the walls of temples and other monuments. Whereas this was once considered "artistic," to leave such graffiti is now the height of bad manners as well as being a criminal offence.

Even those who should know better sometimes engage in acts of vandalism. The poet Lord Byron is amongst those who have left their names carved into the Greek temple at Sounion.

The ancient Greeks interpreted the rustlings of leaves on a sacred oak tree as signs from the gods.

An impression of ancient Athens showing the Parthenon, the temple of Athena, standing high on the Acropolis

A jar showing Tantalus, who stole from the gods and was punished by the mighty Zeus

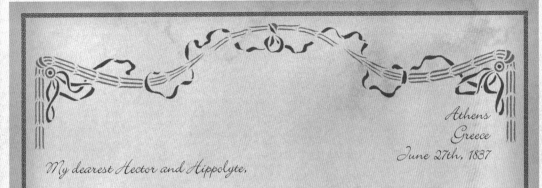

Athens
Greece
June 27th, 1837

My dearest Hector and Hippolyte,

    I hope this letter finds you both well. It saddens me to say that I will not be joining you next week as we had hoped, because my research in Greece is taking much longer than I had anticipated. I miss you terribly, my darlings, and I promise that I will do everything I can to return home as soon as possible. I have been thinking about you every day and have prepared this book for you so that you may grow to love the wondrous myths of the ancient Greeks just as I do.

    The Greek myths date back more than two thousand years and come from a world very different from the one we live in today. Although the ancient Greeks lived in cities — and could read and write, build stone houses, and do basic metalwork — they lacked the modern conveniences to which we are accustomed. They lived in a world that was much closer to the forces of nature than ours, and their myths reflect this simpler way of life.

    Throughout this book I have laid out several activities to keep you amused, and upon my return I shall check your progress! If you have done well, as I am certain you will, then perhaps you may accompany me on my next visit to foreign parts.

               God keep you safe, my dearest ones,
                    Your very affectionate mama

The mighty Titan Cronus had a sickle made of adamant, believed by the ancient Greeks to be the hardest substance in the world.

CONTENTS

The Muses were nine goddesses who assisted writers and musicians.

A Hymn of Praise to the Gods and Muses

I shall begin with the Muses, Apollo, and Zeus,
for it is through the Muses and Apollo
that there are singers upon the Earth and players upon the lyre,
but kings are from Zeus.
Happy is he whom the Muses love; sweet songs flow from his lips!
Hail, children of Zeus!
Give honour to my song!

SECTION I
THE IMMORTALS

THE GODS AND GODDESSES
OF ANCIENT GREECE

The ancient Greeks believed that the world was ruled by the gods, a group of immortal beings who had existed long before mankind. Some Greek myths tell of the origins of the gods and their early struggles; other myths explain the various relationships and rivalries among them.

At first, these myths were passed on by word of mouth, and it was not until much later that they were written down by poets such as Homer and Hesiod. Therefore, it is not altogether surprising that there is a certain amount of confusion and uncertainty about some of the myths.

However, thanks to the work of scholars—your humble mother included—it is now possible to present a clear account of these immortals and their role in the ancient Greek world.

LESSON I
THE TWELVE OLYMPIANS

THE ANCIENT GREEKS believed their gods to be superhuman beings with extraordinary powers and abilities. But the gods were also believed to have powerful human emotions, such as love, jealousy, and anger. There were twelve chief gods—the Olympians—who the ancient Greeks imagined lived at the top of the tallest mountain in the land, Mount Olympus. Looking down from Olympus, the gods could see the whole Earth, and they often interfered in human affairs. Each god or goddess had an individual personality, a different area of responsibility, and certain symbols by which he or she was represented. The relationships between the twelve Olympian gods were very complicated and not always friendly.

ZEUS

Zeus was the king of the gods (as well as the father of some of them). He was also the god of the sky and storms.
SYMBOLS: Eagle, thunderbolt
PARENTS: Cronus and Rhea
APPEARANCE: Crowned; carried a sceptre
CONSORT: Hera (and others)

HERA

The queen of the gods, as well as the goddess of marriage and the heavens, Hera was married to her brother Zeus.
SYMBOLS: Peacock, cow, crow
PARENTS: Cronus and Rhea
APPEARANCE: Crowned; carried a sceptre
CONSORT: Zeus

DEMETER

The goddess of the harvest and fertility, Demeter was responsible for the well-being of crops and farms.

SYMBOLS: Sheaf of wheat, torch
PARENTS: Cronus and Rhea
APPEARANCE: Carried a wheat sheaf
CONSORT: None

ATHENA

The goddess of wisdom, crafts, and war, Athena was the chief goddess of Athens, which is named after her.

SYMBOLS: Owl
PARENTS: Zeus and Metis
APPEARANCE: Wore a helmet; carried a spear and a shield
CONSORT: None

POSEIDON

The god of the sea and of earthquakes, Poseidon was thought to be a bad-tempered old man.

SYMBOLS: Dolphin, horse, trident
PARENTS: Cronus and Rhea
APPEARANCE: Old, bearded; carried a trident
CONSORT: Amphitrite

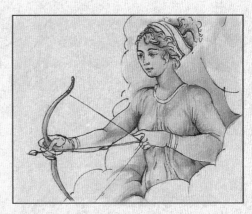

ARTEMIS

The goddess of hunting, the modest Artemis was the protector of animals and young women.

SYMBOLS: Deer, hunting dog
PARENTS: Zeus and Leto
APPEARANCE: Carried a bow and arrows
CONSORT: None

APOLLO

The god of healing, music, poetry, and the sun, Apollo was also the protector of shepherds and the brother of Artemis.

SYMBOLS: Laurel tree, bow, raven, lyre
PARENTS: Zeus and Leto
APPEARANCE: Carried a lyre
CONSORT: No fixed consort

HERMES

The god of travel and trade, Hermes was the messenger of the gods.

SYMBOLS: Caduceus (staff twined with snakes), wings
PARENTS: Zeus and Maia
APPEARANCE: Wore a winged cap and sandals and carried a staff
CONSORT: None

DIONYSUS

The god of wine, agriculture, and celebrations, Dionysus was thought to be a young man with long hair.

SYMBOLS: Vines, ivy
PARENTS: Zeus and Semele
APPEARANCE: Carried grapes, a cup, and a thyrsus (staff)
CONSORT: Ariadne

ARES

The god of war and violence, Ares was thought to be a fierce young warrior.

SYMBOLS: Vulture, dog
PARENTS: Zeus and Hera
APPEARANCE: Dressed for battle (wore a helmet; carried a shield and spear)
CONSORT: None

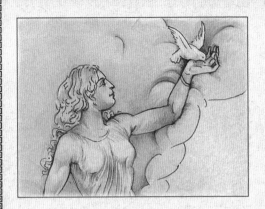

APHRODITE

Aphrodite was a beautiful young woman, the goddess of love and beauty.

SYMBOLS: Dove, apple, seashell

PARENT: Uranus

APPEARANCE: Wore a magic girdle; carried a mirror

CONSORT: Hephaestus

HEPHAESTUS

The god of fire, metalwork, and building, Hephaestus was an ugly, lame old man.

SYMBOLS: Donkey, hammer, anvil

PARENTS: Zeus and Hera

APPEARANCE: Carried a hammer, tongs, and an axe

CONSORT: Aphrodite

ACTIVITY: Can you match the symbols below to their appropriate gods?

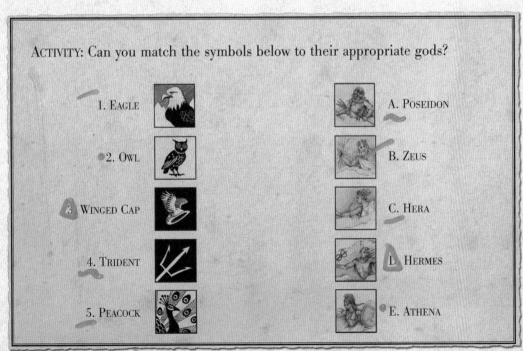

1. EAGLE

2. OWL

3. WINGED CAP

4. TRIDENT

5. PEACOCK

A. POSEIDON

B. ZEUS

C. HERA

D. HERMES

E. ATHENA

LESSON II
OTHER GREEK GODS AND SPIRITS

THE ANCIENT GREEKS believed that many lesser gods and spirits also inhabited and influenced their world. Many of these, such as the god Pan and the nymphs, were closely associated with nature. Others, however, were linked with human passions, such as vengeance or artistic creativity.

THE GOD PAN

Pan was a god of the fields, hills, woodlands, and wild countryside. Half man, half goat, he was renowned for his mischievous, playful personality. He sometimes frightened lone travellers by shouting loudly, so the word *panic* is said to come from his name. His terrible scream also struck terror into the enemies of the gods.

THE FURIES

The Furies were three fearsome, winged goddesses of revenge. They avenged acts of injustice, whether committed by ordinary men, heroes, or the immortal gods. They mercilessly pursued those who broke natural laws, especially the killing of one's own father or mother, and punished such criminals by driving them to madness.

THE MUSES

The Muses (shown left) were daughters of Zeus who inspired humans to be creative. There were nine of these goddesses, and each was associated with a particular activity: Calliope (epic poetry), Clio (history), Erato (love poetry), Euterpe (music), Melpomene (tragedy), Polyhymnia (hymns), Terpsichore (dancing), Thalia (comedy), and Urania (astronomy).

NYMPHS

Nymphs were goddesses of nature. There were several types: dryads were tree nymphs, Nereids were sea nymphs, and naiads were found near rivers and wells.

HESTIA

The goddess Hestia (whose name I have the honour to bear) was once one of the twelve Olympians, but she gave up her place to Dionysus. Hestia was the much-loved goddess of the hearth, home, and family.

When ancient Greek artists and musicians began new works, they would often seek inspiration from the Muses. Sometimes they would compose hymns that thanked and praised the Muses and the gods (especially Zeus and Apollo) for their assistance.

ACTIVITY: Can you name the Muse who would have been associated with each of these symbols?

1.   2.   3.   4.

LESSON III
GREEK MYTHS OF CREATION

THE GREEKS did not have just one myth to describe the beginning of the world; they had several. In the myths recounted by the poet Hesiod, there was originally just the swirling void of Chaos. From Chaos came three beings: Gaia (the goddess of the Earth), Tartarus (the god of the place below the Earth), and Eros (the god of love). Later came Night, Day, and Uranus (the god of the sky). Uranus married Gaia, and together they produced the Titans.

THE TITANS

Uranus feared his Titan children and locked them away in Tartarus. But their mother, Gaia, gave the youngest and fiercest Titan, Cronus, an unbreakable sickle so he could kill his father. Cronus married his sister Rhea, and she gave birth to six of the gods. As his father had, Cronus imprisoned his own children, and these gods had to fight a war against their parents to win control of the world.

THE COSMIC EGG

According to a different series of Greek myths, the world began with a single cosmic egg, which was laid by Time. From this egg emerged a primeval god, variously called Phanes, Protogonos, or Eros — a winged being whose legs were covered with coiling serpents. This god was the first ruler of the universe and gave birth to everything that came afterwards.

THE BIRTH OF APHRODITE

There are also different stories surrounding the origins of individual gods, such as Aphrodite. Some myths say she was the daughter of Zeus and of the goddess Dione. Other myths, however, describe how she was born from the sea to Uranus after he was defeated by Cronus. According to this version, Aphrodite is therefore older than Zeus and the other Olympians.

ACTIVITY: There are many different stories of creation. Use your imagination to write your own myth about how the world and humankind came into being. Try to be as original as possible!

LESSON IV
LIFE ON OLYMPUS

MOUNT OLYMPUS is a tall, snowcapped mountain in eastern Greece. At one time, the ancient Greeks believed that the twelve Olympian gods lived together at the top of this cold, windswept peak in a huge, magnificent palace protected by steep walls.

TROUBLE IN PARADISE

Like any large family, the gods were always bickering amongst themselves. The goddesses were especially jealous of one another. A famous "beauty contest" occurred between Aphrodite, Athena, and Hera. Aphrodite persuaded Paris, a prince of Troy who had been chosen to judge the contest, to select her as the fairest by offering him marriage to Helen, the most beautiful woman in the world. Helen's husband, the proud Greek king Menelaus, was so angered by this that he started the Trojan War.

Paris chooses the fairest goddess.

FOOD AND DRINK

On Olympus, the gods lived in idle luxury, with servants to keep their glasses and plates filled. They feasted on a special food known as ambrosia and drank nectar and wine. Ambrosia and nectar were reserved exclusively for the gods, and Zeus was quick to punish any bold mortals who dared to taste this divine fare.

THRONES OF THE GODS

According to some myths, the gods' palace contained special thrones made of precious materials that were beautifully carved and decorated. Each god sat on a different throne.

← ZEUS

Zeus's throne was the largest, made of polished black marble, decorated with gold, and covered with a purple ram's fleece. A bright blue canopy hung over the throne, and a gold eagle sat on its right arm.

POSEIDON →

Poseidon's throne was the second largest, made of sea-green marble streaked with white. It was decorated with sea creatures, coral, and mother-of-pearl.

ZEUS'S
THRONE

POSEIDON'S
THRONE

← ARTEMIS

Artemis sat on a throne made of silver. The back was shaped like a boat, with a date palm at each side. The image of a she-bear was carved into the throne, and a wolf's skin covered the seat.

APHRODITE →

Aphrodite's throne was also silver and was inlaid with aquamarines, beryls, and other precious stones. The back of the throne was shaped like a large seashell, and the seat was made of soft swansdown.

ARTEMIS'S
THRONE

APHRODITE'S
THRONE

ACTIVITY: Imagine that you are a new god on Olympus. Design your own throne using materials and decorations to suit your powers and personality.

LESSON V
THE UNDERWORLD

THE ANCIENT GREEKS believed that the souls of the dead inhabited the underworld, which they called Hades. It was divided into different regions: the souls of heroes and the virtuous dwelt in the Elysian Fields, the wicked were punished in Tartarus, and those who were neither good nor bad were sent to the plains of Asphodel. The dead were buried with a coin called an *obol* in their mouth as payment for Charon, the ferryman, to row their soul into the underworld across the River Styx.

HADES

The Greeks gave the name *Hades* both to the underworld itself and to the gloomy god who ruled over it. He was stern and unforgiving, presiding over his dark, desolate kingdom. Hades wore a cap of invisibility made for him by the Cyclopes, and he carried a two-pronged spear. No woman would willingly marry the god of the dead, so Hades became very lonely. This led him to kidnap Persephone, daughter of the goddess Demeter.

ETERNAL PUNISHMENTS

Those who committed terrible crimes could expect terrible punishments in Tartarus, and for the worst offenders, the punishments were everlasting. A wicked king named Tantalus was made to stand up to his neck in water with some delicious fruit dangling in front of his mouth. Whenever he tried to eat or drink, the fruit moved out of reach and the water shrank away. This story gave us the word *tantalising*—for something desirable that is just out of reach.

CERBERUS

The god Hades had a monstrous dog called Cerberus: a huge, three-headed beast that was said never to sleep. Cerberus guarded the gates of the underworld, not only stopping the souls of the dead from escaping but also preventing the living from trying to enter and rescue their loved ones from the clutches of death.

THE LIVING AND THE DEAD

Despite the watchful Cerberus, several heroes did manage to enter the underworld and return alive. Orpheus went there to try to rescue his dead wife, and Odysseus went to consult the soul of the blind fortune-teller Tiresias. Heracles, however, went one better. He entered the underworld, captured Cerberus with his bare hands, and took him back to the land of the living.

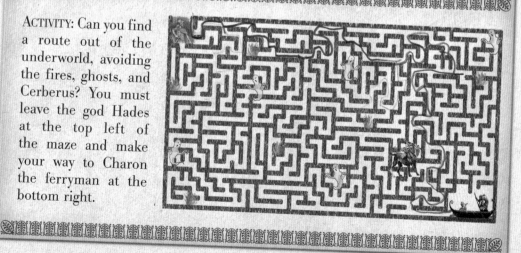

ACTIVITY: Can you find a route out of the underworld, avoiding the fires, ghosts, and Cerberus? You must leave the god Hades at the top left of the maze and make your way to Charon the ferryman at the bottom right.

LESSON VI
HADES AND PERSEPHONE

THERE WAS ONE GODDESS whose name the ancient Greeks dared not speak aloud. She was Persephone, the Queen of the Dead, whom they called simply the Maiden. The hero Odysseus met her in the underworld and referred to her as the Iron Queen because of her cold and unbending manner. Yet Persephone started life as the beautiful young daughter of Zeus and Demeter, and the story of how she became the Queen of the Dead is a sad tale indeed.

THE ABDUCTION OF PERSEPHONE

There were several gods who wanted to marry the beautiful Persephone, so her mother, Demeter, goddess of the harvest, hid her away in a remote place. But one day, while Persephone was out picking flowers, the god of the dead, Hades, appeared from a crack in the ground and carried her down to the underworld.

THE CHANGING SEASONS

Demeter was heartbroken by her daughter's disappearance and roamed the world, searching for her. While she searched, no crops grew and no flowers bloomed. Eventually, she appealed to Zeus, who decreed that Persephone should be returned to the world of the living, provided that she had eaten nothing during her stay in the underworld. Hades, however, did not give Persephone up so easily. He tricked her into eating four pomegranate seeds. This meant that she had to return to Hades for four months every year. And so, each year, when Persephone returns to her mother, the weather is warm, plants grow, and flowers bloom. But during the months when Persephone lives in the underworld as Queen of the Dead, Demeter once again laments her absence and the world experiences the long, harsh months of winter.

Pomegranates were widely grown in ancient Greece, and few people were able to resist the sweet, tangy taste of their brightly coloured seeds.

While Demeter, the goddess of the harvest, searched high and low for her daughter, the land lay dry and barren.

ACTIVITY: The Eleusinian Mysteries were ceremonies held each spring to celebrate the return of Persephone from the underworld. See what you can find out about them.

23

LESSON VII
ENEMIES OF THE GODS

BEFORE THE RULE OF THE TWELVE OLYMPIANS, the Titans controlled the world. They were terrible beings so huge that they used mountains as seats. Cronus's throne was said to be Mount Olympus itself. The gods, led by the thunderbolt-wielding Zeus, fought a great war against the Titans for control of Olympus and the world. During this war, each side was aided by various fierce monsters.

THE TWELVE CHIEF TITANS

Cronus: King of the Titans

Rhea: Queen of the Titans

Oceanus: Titan of the Great Ocean

Tethys: Titaness of the Sea

Coeus: Titan of Intelligence

Mnemosyne: Titaness of Memory

Crius: Titan of the Stars

Phoebe: Titaness of the Moon

Hyperion: Titan of Light; father of the Sun, Moon, and Dawn

Theia: Titaness of Sight; mother of the Sun, Moon, and Dawn

Themis: Titaness of Justice and Order

Iapetus: Titan of Mortalilty; father of Atlas and Prometheus

THE WAR AGAINST THE TITANS

The Greek myths contain many parallels: before there were twelve Olympian gods, there were twelve chief Titans. Like the gods, the Titans divided the world into different areas of responsibility. The offspring of the chief Titans played an important part in the ancient myths, just as the children of the gods did. In the great war between the gods and the Titans, Atlas (the son of Iapetus) commanded the Titan armies against the gods, but his brother Prometheus fought on the side of the gods. After ten years of terrible war, during which the oceans boiled and the Earth itself caught fire, Zeus and his allies defeated the Titans and banished them from the heavens into the darkest depths of Tartarus.

The twelve chief Titans were the children of Uranus and Gaia.

TYPHON

Soon after the Titans had been defeated, another enemy arose to challenge the gods. Typhon was an enormous monster with flaming breath and with writhing snakes for legs. He fathered many beasts, including Cerberus (Hades' dog), the Hydra, and the Nemean Lion. Zeus eventually managed to vanquish Typhon and cast him into Tartarus.

MONSTROUS ALLIES

Fighting on the side of the gods were three giant brothers called the Cyclopes. Each had a single eye in the middle of his forehead. They were skilled metalworkers who forged Zeus's thunderbolts, Poseidon's trident, and Hades' helmet of invisibility. Like the Titans, these Cyclopes were the children of Gaia and Uranus. (Much later came a different race of Cyclopes, who were wild and unruly. This race included Polyphemus, who was slain by Odysseus.) Also fighting for the gods were the Hundred-handers, each with fifty heads and a hundred arms. They threw rocks the size of small mountains at the Titans—a hundred at a time!

A GIGANTIC BATTLE

The Gigantes were a race of fearsome giants who arose from the Earth to make a final attack upon the gods. They piled mountain upon mountain in an attempt to reach the heavens, but the gods managed to defeat them, aided by the hero Heracles.

ACTIVITY: Draw a picture of Zeus and his allies in battle against the Titans. Remember that his favourite weapon was the thunderbolt.

LESSON VIII
RELIGION IN ANCIENT GREECE

THE ANCIENT GREEKS did not have a sacred book, such as the Bible or the Koran; instead, they had an assortment of myths. Everyone learned at least some of the myths in childhood, but only the most learned priests and storytellers knew all the stories.

HYMN TO ZEUS

I WILL SING OF ZEUS, CHIEFEST
AMONG THE GODS AND GREATEST,
ALL-SEEING, THE LORD OF ALL,
THE FULFILLER, WHO WHISPERS
WORDS OF WISDOM TO THEMIS AS
SHE SITS LEANING TOWARDS HIM.
BE GRACIOUS, ALL-SEEING SON OF
CRONUS, MOST EXCELLENT
AND GREAT!

WORSHIP IN ANCIENT GREECE

The ancient Greeks worshipped mainly in temples: buildings that contained a statue of a particular god or goddess. Originally, these statues were carved from wood, but later many were made from stone or even gold or ivory. Each city and district had its own favourite god. In Athens, the main temple was dedicated to Athena, while at Olympia people worshipped Zeus. The Temple of Artemis, at Ephesus, was one of the Seven Wonders of the Ancient World. The gods were worshipped through dances, festivals, dramas, plays, and poetry recitals.

SACRIFICES

The sacrifice of animals is a very ancient form of worship. An ancient Greek family might sacrifice a single chicken or lamb to thank one of the gods or to seek their help. On major public occasions, however, a temple priest would sacrifice as many as a hundred cattle at a time (a sacrifice of a hundred was known as a hecatomb). The crowds then feasted on the meat, while the skin, fat, and bones were burned as an offering to the gods.

FESTIVALS

Each city had at least one great festival every year. First there would be a procession through the streets, usually followed by the recital of hymns in praise of the gods, then other activities such as dramatic recitals or athletic games. Some of the festivals were serious, solemn affairs, whereas others, such as the harvest festivals, were often an excuse for singing, dancing, and general merrymaking.

ACTIVITY: Look at the hymn to Zeus on the opposite page, then write your own to one of the gods or goddesses. It is often a good idea to ask for help from the Muses in the first line of your hymn.

LESSON IX
ANCIENT GREEK ARCHITECTURE

ARCHITECTURE was one of the greatest accomplishments of the ancient Greeks, and their building style has been imitated many times through the ages. Across Greece there are countless ruins of ancient buildings such as temples and theatres, some of which are in surprisingly good condition, considering their great age.

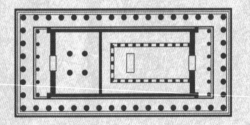

The Parthenon of Athens, completed in 432 BC, was a magnificent temple built to honour the goddess Athena. It is thought to be one of the greatest achievements of ancient Greek architecture.

TEMPLES

Ancient Greek temples, like the statues they contained, were once made entirely of wood. Later, when the Greeks learned how to build with stone, they continued to follow the design of the wooden buildings. A temple usually had a rectangular base (although some were circular) and tall columns that supported the roof. Originally these columns were simply the trunks of trees trimmed of branches, but later these tree trunks, too, were carefully copied in stone.

DORIC   IONIC   CORINTHIAN

THE STYLES OF GREEK COLUMNS

The first stone temples had columns in a plain design called the Doric style. Later, the tops of the columns, called capitals, were carved with spirals in what is known as the Ionic style. Ionic columns also had large bases. Later still, the Corinthian style was adopted, with even more decoration on the capitals.

ANCIENT GREEK THEATRES

As far as we know, the ancient Greeks invented theatres. These structures were semicircular and usually built into a hillside so that the rows of seats could be arranged one above the other around the stage. Simple in design, these theatres paved the way for more elaborate versions by the Romans.

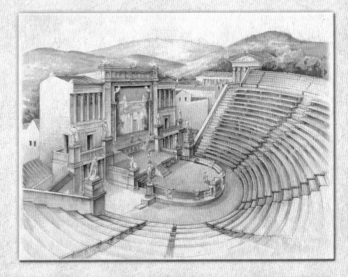

ACTIVITY: In ancient times, the Seven Wonders of the World were widely famous. Can you find out what these wonders were? How many of them were in Greece?

The gods were often thought to interfere in the lives of mortals. Mighty Zeus could send thunderbolts down from the heavens to destroy anyone who angered him.

Even the friendliest gods had fearsome powers: when he was captured by pirates, Dionysus turned them all into dolphins.

During the Trojan War, the goddess Athena pulled Achilles by the hair to prevent him from killing King Agamemnon in a fit of rage.

SECTION II
GODS AND MEN

THE DIVINE AND THE MORTAL

The ancient Greeks believed that during the earliest times, the gods often walked amongst ordinary people, dealing directly with them. Many myths describe these encounters between gods and humans. Meeting a god was a very tricky business because of their immense power. For some people, an encounter with one of the immortals was fatal. At the very best, a person could expect to be sadder but wiser afterwards.

Many of the myths about gods and mortals contain a lesson for the listener, usually about good manners and correct behaviour. So pay close attention to these stories, my dears, for your mama expects to see improvements when she returns!

I WILL TELL OF DIONYSUS AND HOW HE APPEARED BY THE SHORE OF THE SEA. THERE CAME OVER THE SEA TYRRHENIAN PIRATES, WHO SPRANG OUT AND, SEIZING HIM, PUT HIM ON BOARD THEIR SHIP. THEY SOUGHT TO BIND HIM WITH RUDE BONDS, BUT THE BONDS WOULD NOT HOLD HIM, AND HE SAT WITH A SMILE IN HIS DARK EYES. THE HELMSMAN CRIED OUT TO HIS FELLOWS:

"MADMEN! WHAT GOD IS THIS WHOM YOU HAVE TAKEN? HE LOOKS NOT LIKE MORTAL MEN BUT LIKE THE GODS WHO DWELL ON OLYMPUS. LET US SET HIM FREE UPON THE DARK SHORE. DO NOT LAY HANDS ON HIM, LEST HE GROW ANGRY AND STIR UP DANGEROUS WINDS AND STORMS."

— FROM THE HOMERIC HYMN TO DIONYSUS

LESSON X
MYTHICAL CREATURES

A WIDE VARIETY OF fabulous creatures and terrible beasts populated the Greek myths. A few of them were helpful and made the world a better place, but most were hostile. The Greeks told many tales of mighty heroes who vanquished these savage beasts. Other stories tell of helpful creatures, such as Pegasus, who was elevated to the heavens.

PEGASUS

Pegasus was a flying steed tamed and ridden by the hero Bellerophon, who used a magic bridle given to him by the goddess Athena.

FORM: Winged horse

ORIGIN: Arose from the blood of Medusa, the mortal Gorgon

WEAPONS: None

FATE: Turned into a constellation

THE SATYRS

These wild, hairy creatures of the forest were often found revelling with the god Dionysus.

FORM: Half man, half goat, often with small horns

ORIGIN: Natural spirits

WEAPONS: Music and merrymaking

FATE: Believed by some to still exist

ECHIDNA

Echidna was the consort of Typhon and is often referred to as the Mother of All Monsters.

FORM: Half beautiful nymph, half huge and fearsome serpent

ORIGIN: Offspring of the ancient sea god Phorkys and the sea monster Keto

WEAPONS: The strong coils of her serpentine body

FATE: Killed by Hera's watchman, Argus, the hundred-eyed giant

THE GORGONS

These three unspeakably horrible sisters had long fangs and a mass of hissing snakes for hair.

FORM: Roughly human with golden wings, snakes for hair, and hands of copper

ORIGIN: Offspring of Phorkys and Keto, two of the Gorgons were immortal, while one, Medusa, was mortal.

WEAPONS: Their appearance turned people to stone.

FATE: Medusa was killed by the hero Perseus.

THE HARPIES

These vicious flying creatures tormented humans and could swoop down to steal whatever they pleased, chiefly food.

FORM: Half woman, half bird

ORIGIN: Daughters of the Nereid (sea nymph) Electra and the sea god of wonders, Thaumas

WEAPONS: Strong, clawlike hands

FATE: Exiled to the island of Crete by the Argonauts

THE MINOTAUR

This man-eating monster was kept imprisoned in a labyrinth in Crete beneath the palace of King Minos.

FORM: The body of a man with a bull's head

ORIGIN: Son of Queen Pasiphaë of Crete

WEAPONS: Great strength, bull's horns

FATE: Killed by the hero Theseus

THE CHIMERA

The Chimera was a three-headed, fire-spitting monster that roamed the ancient district of Lycia (in present-day Turkey).

FORM: A lion with a goat's head on its back and a snake's or dragon's head on its tail

ORIGIN: Offspring of Typhon and Echidna

WEAPONS: Claws, horns, fangs, fire

FATE: Killed by the hero Bellerophon

THE HYDRA

This formidable serpent had poisonous breath and many heads. If one of its heads was cut off, it could grow two new ones.

FORM: Each head had a long, flexible neck.

ORIGIN: Offspring of Typhon and Echidna

WEAPONS: Poisonous fangs and breath

FATE: Killed by the hero Heracles, with the help of Iolaus, his nephew

SCYLLA

Scylla was a six-headed monster that lived on one side of the narrow channel of sea between Sicily and Italy. On the other side was Charybdis, a monstrous whirlpool.

FORM: Six-headed, with twelve legs

ORIGIN: Was once a Nereid but was turned into a monster after incurring the wrath of the sorceress Circe

WEAPONS: Vast size and many teeth

FATE: Turned into a rock

THE CYCLOPES

Unlike their peaceful predecessors who were descended from Gaia and Uranus, these evil, man-eating giants killed and ate unfortunate seafarers who landed on Sicily.

FORM: Tall and strong, with a single eye

ORIGIN: Offspring of the sea god, Poseidon

WEAPONS: Sticks and stones

FATE: The hero Odysseus blinded the Cyclops Polyphemus in order to escape from his cave.

LADON

This dragon that never slept was the guardian of the beautiful garden of the Hesperides, where golden apples grew.

FORM: Fearsome and scaly

ORIGIN: Offspring of Phorkys and Keto

WEAPONS: Many heads

FATE: Killed by the hero Heracles

THE SPHINX

This flying female tormented travellers in Greece with a riddle. She killed and ate those who could not give the correct answer.

FORM: The head and shoulders of a woman with the body of a winged lion

ORIGIN: Offspring of Typhon and Echidna according to some myths, of Orthus and the Chimera according to others

WEAPONS: "Impossible" riddle

FATE: Killed herself when the hero Oedipus gave the correct answer to the riddle

---

ACTIVITY: Ancient Greek monsters were often a combination of different creatures. Design and draw your own monster, give it a name, and invent a hero who is able to defeat it.

LESSON XI
THE HISTORY OF MANKIND

THE GREEK MYTHS are unclear about the origin of human beings. According to one myth, the god Zeus created the first people. In another myth, the Titan Prometheus, who had fought on the side of the gods against the other Titans, made the first people out of clay.

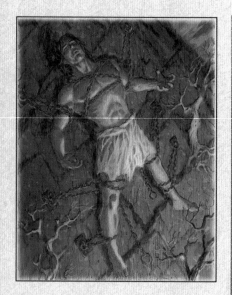

A BOX OF TROUBLES

In order to punish mankind for having received the stolen gift of fire, Zeus ordered Hephaestus to create Pandora, the first woman. Aphrodite made her attractive, Athena taught her needlework, and Hermes gave her insatiable curiosity. The gods also gave her a closed box with strict instructions never, ever to open it. But Pandora's curiosity got the better of her—she opened the box and released all the troubles of the world: disease, despair, vice, violence, cruelty, plague, famine, and old age. Pandora quickly slammed the lid shut again, keeping only the spirit of hope inside.

THE SECRET OF FIRE

The ancient myths tell that Prometheus stole the secret of fire from Mount Olympus and gave it to mankind. This angered Zeus, who ordered that Prometheus be bound in chains to a mountain. Each day, a savage eagle would come and rip out his liver, which would regrow each night. After a few hundred years of this torture, the hero Heracles rescued Prometheus.

THE AGES OF MANKIND

The ancient Greeks believed that human history could be divided into different periods, or ages, which were symbolised by different metals.

THE GOLDEN AGE

The first period of human history was the Golden Age, in which men and gods lived together and were at peace. People did not have to work hard to feed themselves, because wild food was plentiful.

THE SILVER AGE

During the Silver Age, it was said that people lived for a hundred years as children. They spent only a short time as adults before they died. They refused to worship the gods and so were destroyed by an angry Zeus.

THE BRONZE AGE

The Bronze Age was a time of constant and unrelenting warfare. People lived in bronze houses and fought one another with bronze weapons. Eventually they became victims of their own violent ways and destroyed themselves.

THE IRON AGE

The ancient Greeks believed that they were living during the Iron Age: a time of hardship and grief, endless toil and misery, when honour and truth were forgotten.

ACTIVITY: The ancient Greek writer Hesiod described another age between the Bronze and Iron Ages called the Heroic Age. See what you can find out about the Heroic Age.

LESSON XII
MYTHICAL PEOPLES

THE ANCIENT GREEKS BELIEVED that their world was inhabited not only by humans but by several other intelligent races. Among the peoples described in various myths are the Amazons, the centaurs, and numerous kinds of giants.

THE AMAZONS

The Amazons were a race of female warriors who lived on the shores of the Black Sea. They were fierce, proud, fearless in battle, and bitter enemies of the Greeks. Armies of Amazons often attacked Greek settlements in the land that we now know as Turkey. The best known of the Amazons was Queen Hippolyte, who possessed a magic girdle, or belt, that was given to her by her father, the war god, Ares. Another famous Amazonian queen was Penthesilea, who was killed outside the walls of Troy by the hero Achilles when she led her army against the Greeks in support of the besieged Trojans.

THE CENTAURS

The centaurs had the torso, arms, and head of a man on a horse's four-legged body. They were a wild and uncivilised people who were skilled with weapons and generally hostile towards humans. An exception was Chiron, a wise tutor who befriended and taught several Greek heroes, including Theseus, Achilles, and Heracles.

THE GIANTS

The only "friendly" giants in the Greek myths were Arges, Brontes, and Steropes, the Cyclopes who fought on the side of the gods against the Titans. All the other giants, such as the Gigantes, who rose up against the gods, were decidedly hostile. Some of these giants were associated with sea journeys. Polyphemus the Cyclops, for example, was a man-eating giant who preyed on seafarers who landed on his island. The giants of Laestrygonia ate humans and threw rocks at passing Greek ships, including that of the hero Odysseus, who only narrowly escaped their attack.

MAP OF THE LOCATION OF MYTHICAL PEOPLES AND BEASTS

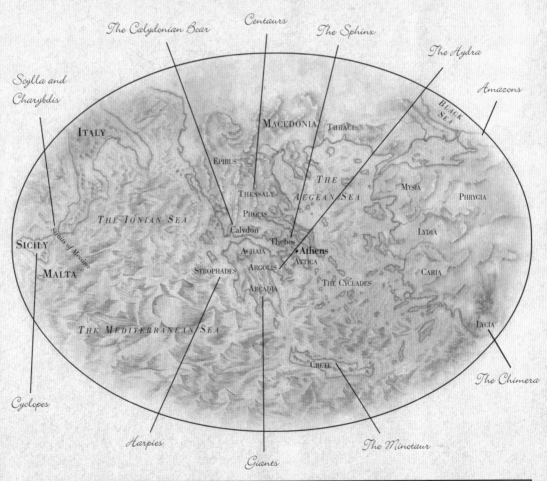

ACTIVITY: A map of ancient Greece appears above. Using a modern atlas, can you find the present-day names of the countries and islands that surround Greece?

LESSON XIII
THE WANDERINGS OF DIONYSUS

DURING THE GOLDEN AGE, when mortals and gods shared the world, it was the god of wine, Dionysus, who spent the most time wandering amongst humans. His followers included a group of women called Maenads, meaning "wild ones." They were thought to dance frenziedly through the countryside, wearing animal skins and wreaths of vine leaves and intoxicated by wine. Wine was very important to the ancient Greeks, although they usually drank it mixed with water to lessen its effects.

A group of Maenads make a wine offering to Dionysus.

SEMELE AND THE BIRTH OF DIONYSUS

Dionysus was the son of Zeus and of a mortal named Semele. The goddess Hera was jealous when she heard that Zeus had married Semele. She disguised herself and befriended Semele, then planted seeds of doubt in Semele's mind, asking if she had any proof of her husband's godly status. In this way, Hera tricked Semele into demanding to see Zeus in his true form, wreathed in lightning. Semele was burned up by the sight. However, Zeus was able to protect his unborn son, Dionysus, by sewing him into his thigh and giving birth when the time was right.

DIONYSUS'S EARLY LIFE

A kindly old man named Silenus supervised Dionysus's upbringing and later became one of his followers. He taught Dionysus to grow grapevines, and together they discovered how to turn the grapes into wine. When Dionysus grew up, Hera, still angry and jealous, struck him with madness. In this state, he roamed the world until he was cured by the goddess Rhea. Dionysus continued to travel, passing on the wisdom of wine making. He is said to have voyaged as far as India.

DIONYSUS AND THE PIRATES

On one of Dionysus's journeys, some pirates made the mistake of capturing him. The god turned their oars into snakes and filled their ship with vines. He then changed himself into a lion and chased the pirates overboard, where they were turned into dolphins.

Silenus was a lover of wine and often had to be carried on the back of a donkey.

ACTIVITY: Go to page 77, which shows the names of the gods in Greek.

Can you find Dionysus's name in this grid?

How many other names of gods and goddesses can you find? They can be read up, down, forwards, backwards, or diagonally.

Α	Θ	Η	Ν	Α	Ζ	Θ	Δ
Κ	Ρ	Ρ	Ε	Σ	Τ	Ι	Α
Ψ	Π	Α	Ν	Ω	Ο	Κ	Π
Δ	Υ	Β	Χ	Ν	Λ	Α	Ο
Ζ	Λ	Π	Υ	Ω	Ρ	Ε	Λ
Ε	Α	Σ	Ο	Η	Θ	Ι	Λ
Υ	Ο	Ρ	Σ	Η	Δ	Α	Ω
Σ	Υ	Τ	Γ	Ω	Ψ	Β	Ν

LESSON XIV
ANCIENT GREEK ART

THE ARTISTIC STYLES of the ancient Greeks have had a strong influence on artists throughout history. Most of what we know about ancient Greek art comes from statues and carvings found in ruined temples or from coins and vases excavated from the ground. Sadly, many ancient Greek treasures have been lost, and some of the surviving "Greek" artworks are, in fact, copies made by the Romans.

The owl on her shield identifies this statue as depicting the goddess Athena.

Temples were often decorated with carved figures, such as this centaur.

PORTRAYING THE GODS

Greek statues varied in size from small tabletop figurines to large figures for open-air display. They were usually carved from stone, such as marble, or made of bronze. The gods and goddesses were favourite subjects of Greek sculptors, whether they chose to portray Athena sitting in splendour as protector of a city or Aphrodite casually adjusting her sandal strap. The most gifted sculptors (such as Phidias, who supervised the building of the Parthenon, in Athens) became famous throughout the Greek world. They were highly sought after to produce work of all types, from great statues for temples to small designs on coins.

PAINTED POTS

Ancient Greek cookware was plain and undecorated, but the tableware used at banquets was often crafted from precious metals or painted with exquisite pictures of gods and heroes. The images below show modern replicas of ancient-Greek-style vases.

CRATERS

Two-handled, wide-mouthed bowls such as the ones shown above are called craters. They would have been used by the ancient Greeks to dilute wine with water at feasts. The crater on the left shows a scene from the story of Tantalus, who stole the delicious ambrosia of the gods, thereby incurring the wrath of Zeus. The central crater shows Poseidon and Amphitrite in their chariot, while the crater on the right shows a battle between Greek and Trojan warriors.

AMPHORAS

This type of vase, called an amphora, was used to hold wine or oil. Like craters, amphoras had two handles so that they could be carried easily, but they had narrower necks than craters. This example, with a decorative border, shows the goddess Demeter carrying a sheaf of wheat.

A DRINKER'S VIEW

The insides of some pottery items were decorated as well as their outsides. Seen from above, the inside of this drinking cup is painted with various mythical creatures, including the Minotaur and a centaur.

ACTIVITY: Design your own Greek-style vase and decorate it with a scene from one of your favourite myths.

LESSON XV
DAEDALUS AND ICARUS

DAEDALUS WAS AN ANCIENT GREEK artist and inventor supposedly born in Athens, and Icarus was his son. Historians do not agree as to whether Daedalus actually existed or not. The tales told about him are too fantastic to be entirely true, but it is possible that they were based on the life of a real person.

THE FLIGHT OF DAEDALUS AND ICARUS

Daedalus was employed by King Minos of Crete to design and construct an inescapable maze, called the Labyrinth, to imprison the monstrous Minotaur. Once the Labyrinth was finished, Minos wanted to be sure that nobody would learn its secrets, so he forbade Daedalus from leaving Crete. When Minos blocked his escape by land and sea, Daedalus realised that fleeing through the sky was his only option. Using feathers stuck together with wax, he made two pairs of wings: one for himself and one for Icarus. Before taking off, Daedalus warned Icarus not to fly too close to the sun. But Icarus ignored his father's warning and flew higher and higher, until the heat of the sun melted the wax. The wings came apart, and young Icarus fell to his death in the sea.

KING MINOS'S RIDDLE

Daedalus landed safely and went into hiding at the court of King Cocalus in Sicily. King Minos was furious that Daedalus had escaped, and he searched high and low for him. He planned to find out Daedalus's whereabouts by circulating a seemingly impossible puzzle: Minos offered a reward to anyone who could thread a length of thin twine through the internal spirals of a seashell. He knew that Daedalus was the only man clever enough to find a solution.

DAEDALUS'S NARROW ESCAPE

Indeed, Daedalus's answer was to drill a small hole in the centre of the shell, glue one end of the twine to an ant, and use honey around the hole to attract the ant from the lip of the shell through the coils to the centre. When Minos heard that someone at the court of Cocalus had solved the riddle, he sent soldiers to surround the palace and demanded that Daedalus be handed over. Cocalus pretended to agree but persuaded Minos to have a bath first. Then Cocalus's daughters poured boiling water on Minos, thus killing him.

ACTIVITY:
Find your way to the middle of the Labyrinth.

Next, draw your own maze with a monster at the centre.

See if any of your friends can find their way to the centre, then back out again to safety.

LESSON XVI
THE HEAVENS

THE GREEKS placed great value on astronomy, which was the only science with its own Muse, Urania. Greek astronomers found patterns of stars in the night sky, called constellations, which they named after figures from myth. As the Earth moves around the sun, the sun seems to move across the sky. Ancient astronomers noticed that it appeared to pass in front of twelve constellations, which they called the zodiac.

ARIES, THE RAM   ΚΡΙΟΣ

Aries was the ram with the Golden Fleece, which was sought by Jason and his Argonauts.

TAURUS, THE BULL   ΤΑΥΡΟΣ

The great god Zeus was said to have turned himself into a bull to kidnap the beautiful princess Europa. She climbed onto his back, and he ran away with her.

GEMINI, THE TWINS   ΑΔΙΔΥΜΟΙ

Castor and Polydeuces were brothers who sailed with Jason on his quest for the Golden Fleece.

CANCER, THE CRAB   ΚΑΡΚΙΝΟΣ

When Heracles fought the Hydra, Hera sent a crab to distract him. It bit his big toe but ultimately failed in its mission, because Heracles crushed it with his foot.

LEO, THE LION   ΑΕΩΝ

Although there were several lions in Greek mythology, Leo represents the Nemean Lion killed by Heracles.

VIRGO, THE VIRGIN ΠΑΡΘΕΝΟΣ

According to some, Virgo was Astraea, the daughter of Zeus and Themis. However, elsewhere Virgo is identified as Persephone, the Maiden.

LIBRA, THE SCALES ΖΥΓΟΣ

These are the scales of justice associated with the goddesses of justice, Themis and her daughter Astraea.

SCORPIO, THE SCORPION ΣΚΟΡΠΙΟΣ

The scorpion represents the creature sent by Artemis to kill the hunter Orion in order to disprove the hero's boast that he could kill every animal on Earth.

SAGITTARIUS, THE ARCHER ΤΟΞΟΤΗΣ

Sagittarius is a centaur holding a drawn bow. This constellation is usually identified with the wise centaur Chiron, who is firing an arrow at nearby Scorpio.

CAPRICORN, THE SHE-GOAT ΑΙΓΟΚΕΡΩΣ

The ancient Greeks believed that Capricorn was the she-goat Amaltheia, who suckled the baby Zeus. He placed her among the stars to honour her.

AQUARIUS, THE WATER CARRIER ΥΔΡΟΧΟΟΣ

Aquarius was thought to represent Ganymede, a handsome Trojan youth taken to Olympus to pour drinks for the gods.

PISCES, THE FISH ΙΧΘΥΕΣ

Aphrodite and her son changed themselves into fish in order to jump into a river and escape from the monster Typhon. They tied themselves together so that they would not become separated.

ACTIVITY: Find out about the best ways of locating constellations in the night sky. Wait for a clear, dark night, then see if you can find any of the constellations above. You might also be able to find some other shapes among the stars!

LESSON XVII
THE LEGEND OF MIDAS

THE STORY OF MIDAS, the king of Phrygia, is a classic cautionary tale about being careful of what you wish for, especially where the gods are concerned. Midas's unfortunate involvement with the gods actually began with an act of kindness.

Midas and Silenus

THE GOLDEN TOUCH

One day, Silenus, the tutor of Dionysus, drank too much wine and became separated from his friends. He staggered around, lost, until he fell into a drunken sleep. Silenus was discovered by some of King Midas's servants. Midas took care of Silenus for ten days and arranged for him to be reunited with Dionysus. The god was so pleased to see his old friend safe and well that he promised to grant Midas a single wish. Midas had always been greedy for riches, so he wished that everything he touched would turn to gold.

FROM BLESSING TO CURSE

The wish was granted, and at first Midas was delighted with his new powers: he sat on golden chairs and lay on a golden bed. But he began to realise his mistake when he discovered that all food and drink turned to gold as soon as it touched his lips, so he became very hungry and thirsty. Midas begged Dionysus to remove the power, and the god kindly agreed.

A MUSIC CONTEST

Midas then chose to avoid riches by moving to the country. He became a follower of the god Pan, and he greatly admired the god's flute playing. One day Pan challenged Apollo to a music contest, and Midas found himself in the audience. Pan played very well, but the melodies that Apollo produced on his lyre were even more beautiful. Apollo was judged the winner by everyone except Midas, who loudly proclaimed that he thought Pan the better musician. Apollo was so angry that he turned Midas's ears into those of a donkey.

Apollo and Pan

DONKEY'S EARS

Midas became extremely shy and embarrassed about his new ears and always wore a pointed hat to hide them. The only other person who knew about them was Midas's barber, who was sworn to secrecy. Unfortunately, the barber could not bear to keep quiet about the ears, so he dug a hole in the ground and whispered the secret into the hole before filling it in. Soon reeds grew up from the hole and whispered the secret to the grass, which whispered it to the trees, which whispered it to the birds, which sang it out across the land. Soon, the whole of Greece had heard that King Midas had big, hairy ears!

ACTIVITY: Imagine that you were granted a wish by a Greek god. What would you wish for? Think of the ways in which it could go wrong. For example, the Delphic Sybil, a prophetess, asked Apollo for eternal life but forgot to ask for eternal youth, so she grew ever older and more wrinkled.

LESSON XVIII
THREE LEGENDS: ORPHEUS, NARCISSUS, AND SISYPHUS

MIDAS WAS NOT THE ONLY CHARACTER in Greek mythology who had a bad encounter with the gods. Orpheus dared to barter with Hades to return his dead wife, while Sisyphus tried a similar trick with Persephone. And selfish Narcissus was punished by the gods for his vanity.

LOST LOVE

Orpheus was a wonderful musician, as was to be expected from the son of Apollo and Calliope, the Muse of epic poetry. His playing was so beautiful that even the animals, trees, and rocks listened to his songs. He fell in love with a nymph named Eurydice, but on their wedding day she was killed by a serpent bite. The heartbroken musician ventured down to the underworld and begged Hades to allow his wife to return to the surface. Orpheus played so beautifully that Hades' hard heart was softened, and he agreed to let Eurydice leave, on one condition: she would follow Orpheus out of the underworld, but if he doubted this and looked back at her, she would vanish. When they had nearly reached the upper world, Orpheus so longed to see that his wife was safe that he stole a glance behind him. In that moment, Eurydice vanished and was lost to him forever. Orpheus failed to live up to his word in a bargain with a god, and he paid dearly for it.

UNREQUITED LOVE

Narcissus was a handsome young man who attracted many admiring glances. The nymph Echo fell in love with him, but he cruelly ignored her, leaving her to gradually fade away until only her voice, an echo, was left. As a punishment, the gods made Narcissus fall hopelessly in love with his own reflection. He sat by the edge of a pool, unable even to eat or drink, trying to get his reflection in the water to talk to him, but it never did. Eventually he died of a broken heart.

PUNISHMENT WITHOUT END

Sisyphus was a clever, arrogant man who stirred up trouble for Zeus. When Zeus sent him to the underworld as a punishment, Sisyphus outwitted the god of death, Thanatos, and tricked Persephone into letting him return to the upper world, as he claimed that the proper burial rites hadn't been performed on his body. Zeus was so angry at this lack of respect for the gods that he sentenced Sisyphus to an everlasting torment in Tartarus. For the rest of time, Sisyphus would strain to push an enormous boulder up a hill, only to have it roll down again when he neared the top.

ACTIVITY: Imagine that you are the god Hades. What eternal punishments can you think of to keep people busy in Tartarus?

The hero Heracles wore the impenetrable skin of the Nemean Lion, which he had killed with his bare hands.

Gods and mortal kings took equal delight in sending heroes on seemingly impossible quests. The hero Jason (above) was sent to fetch the Golden Fleece from the distant land of Colchis, where it was kept under close guard by a dragon that never slept.

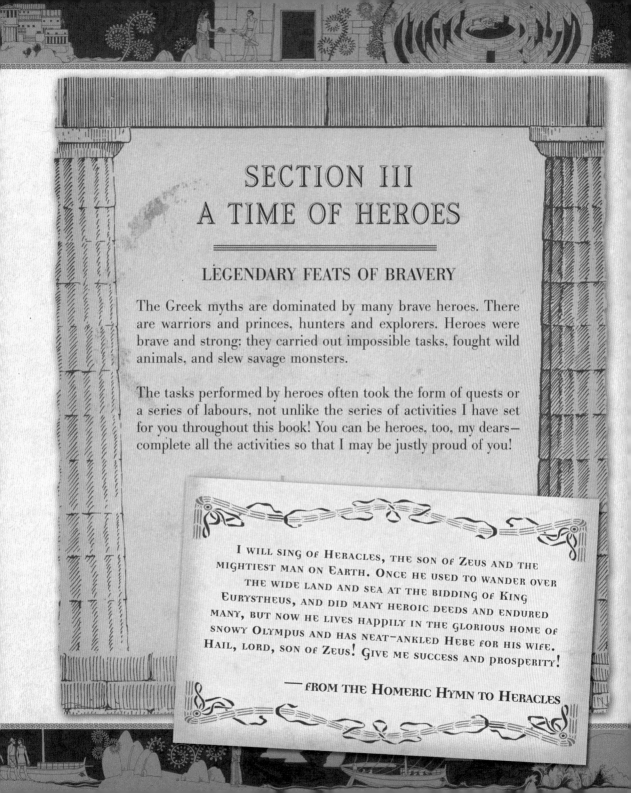

SECTION III
A TIME OF HEROES

LEGENDARY FEATS OF BRAVERY

The Greek myths are dominated by many brave heroes. There are warriors and princes, hunters and explorers. Heroes were brave and strong: they carried out impossible tasks, fought wild animals, and slew savage monsters.

The tasks performed by heroes often took the form of quests or a series of labours, not unlike the series of activities I have set for you throughout this book! You can be heroes, too, my dears—complete all the activities so that I may be justly proud of you!

I WILL SING OF HERACLES, THE SON OF ZEUS AND THE MIGHTIEST MAN ON EARTH. ONCE HE USED TO WANDER OVER THE WIDE LAND AND SEA AT THE BIDDING OF KING EURYSTHEUS, AND DID MANY HEROIC DEEDS AND ENDURED MANY, BUT NOW HE LIVES HAPPILY IN THE GLORIOUS HOME OF SNOWY OLYMPUS AND HAS NEAT-ANKLED HEBE FOR HIS WIFE. HAIL, LORD, SON OF ZEUS! GIVE ME SUCCESS AND PROSPERITY!

— FROM THE HOMERIC HYMN TO HERACLES

LESSON XIX
ANCIENT GREEK HEROES

ANCIENT GREEK HEROES were people who were endowed with exceptional qualities that allowed them to perform great feats of skill or strength. Some heroes were the children of gods, while others had royal blood. Despite their illustrious ancestries, their achievements, and their fame, these heroes rarely had happy lives, and some of them endured great suffering.

HERACLES

The most celebrated of all the Greek heroes, Heracles was the son of the god Zeus and of the beautiful mortal queen Alcmene. Hera hated Heracles because he was the child of one of Zeus's other wives, so while he was still a baby, she sent two huge snakes to kill him. Young Heracles strangled both serpents and grew up to be a man of immense strength. He performed many daring feats, including the twelve labours for which he is most famous. After Heracles' death, Zeus made him immortal.

THESEUS

Theseus was a hero of Athens. Some say he was the son of Poseidon, others say the son of Aegeus, king of Athens. He was raised in the city of Troezen by his mother, Aethra. Theseus performed his most famous feat when he travelled to Crete to try to defeat the Minotaur. The creature (half bull, half man) lived in a maze called the Labyrinth, from which no one could escape. Aided by King Minos's daughter, Ariadne, who gave Theseus a ball of string, the hero found his way through the Labyrinth and slew the Minotaur with the sword of Aegeus.

JASON

Jason was the rightful king of the city of Iolcus, but the power-hungry Pelias had overthrown Jason's father and now ruled unlawfully. Pelias sent Jason to fetch the famous Golden Fleece from the land of Colchis, thinking it an impossible task from which he would never return. Jason built a ship named the *Argo* and, with a crew of fifty heroes, set sail for Colchis. After many adventures, Jason and his "Argonauts" succeeded in their quest, but only with the help of Hera and the sorceress Medea.

THE DIOSCURI

The Dioscuri ("sons of Zeus") were the twins Castor and Polydeuces, one of whom was mortal, the other immortal. The mortal Castor was an excellent horseman, while the immortal Polydeuces was a champion boxer. The brothers accompanied Jason on the *Argo*. Afterwards, they argued with their cousins about the ownership of a cow, and Castor was killed. Polydeuces begged Zeus to let him share his immortality with his brother, and Zeus agreed, so together the twins spend a day in heaven, followed by a day in Hades.

PERSEUS

This hero killed the Gorgon Medusa by cutting off her head. Although Perseus was a great warrior, he could accomplish this feat only with the assistance of the immortals. The goddess Athena gave him a mirrorlike shield that he could use to look at Medusa without being turned to stone. The god Hermes gave him a magic sword, and some nymphs gave him a helmet that made him invisible, a purse, and a pair of winged shoes.

ACHILLES

The most heroic warrior of the Trojan War, Achilles was dipped into the River Styx as a baby so that no weapons could harm him. His only vulnerable place was his heel, where his mother had held him as she lowered him into the water. Achilles was unbeatable in battle, and he helped the Greeks win the war. However, he did not live to see the victory. The Trojan prince Paris killed him by shooting an arrow straight into his heel after Achilles killed Paris's brother Hector.

ODYSSEUS

Clever Odysseus was said to rival Achilles as a warrior, but his most famous adventures began at the end of the Trojan War. The gods who had supported the Trojans decided to punish Odysseus by making his journey home last for ten years. He and his crew endured storms and shipwreck, were turned into pigs by the enchantress Circe, and were drawn off course by the song of the Sirens. When Odysseus finally did get home, he had to defeat more than a hundred rivals in order to regain his throne.

ATALANTA

Atalanta was the daughter of an ancient Greek king. When she was a baby, her father abandoned her in a remote forest. Luckily, Atalanta was found and brought up by a she-bear, and later a group of hunters looked after her. She was an athletic young woman, skilled with bow and arrow, and she became a famous huntress. In one version of the myth, Jason wanted Atalanta to join the Argonauts but would not allow her to because having a woman on board was considered bad luck.

ORION

Orion was the son of the sea god, Poseidon. He was a mighty hunter who single-handedly rid the island of Chios of wild beasts. He was invited to Crete to go hunting with the goddess Artemis herself. According to one version of the story, Eos, the goddess of the dawn, was also there, and she fell in love with Orion. Artemis became quite jealous and "accidentally" killed Orion with an arrow from her bow. Another version of the myth says that Artemis sent a scorpion to sting him.

CADMUS

Cadmus was a foreign prince whose sister, Europa, was kidnapped by Zeus. He set out to Greece to find her, and there he was attacked by a dragon sent by the god Ares. Cadmus killed the dragon and was instructed by Athena to sow the dragon's teeth in the ground. From the ground then sprang an army of warriors. Cadmus threw a stone amongst them, tricking them into fighting and destroying one another. He later married Harmonia, the daughter of Ares and Aphrodite.

OEDIPUS

This hero had a most unfortunate story that made him the central character in several Greek dramas. Through a combination of bad luck and bad temper, he unknowingly killed his father and then married his mother to become king of Thebes. When he discovered what he had done, he was so sorrowful and angry that he plucked out his own eyes. He spent the rest of his life wandering through Greece as a blind beggar.

ORPHEUS

Orpheus was a gifted musician who was one of Jason's Argonauts. During the voyage to find the Golden Fleece, his lyre playing helped to soothe the tensions between the various proud heroes. After the death of his wife, Eurydice, Orpheus went to live by himself in the mountains. His presence there aroused the anger of a group of crazed Maenads, and they killed him. His lyre was placed in the heavens as a constellation, and he was allowed to live in the Elysian Fields in the underworld.

ACTIVITY: Can you match these heroes with the god or goddess who had an influence on them?
1. Jason 2. Cadmus 3. Orion 4. The Dioscuri
A. Zeus B. Artemis C. Athena D. Hera

LESSON XX
THE LABOURS OF HERACLES

THROUGHOUT MOST OF HIS LIFE, Heracles had to endure torments from the jealous goddess Hera. After he married a princess of Thebes, Heracles was driven mad by Hera and, in a fit of rage, killed his wife and six of his children. To make amends for this terrible crime, Heracles was sent into the service of Eurystheus, the king of Mycenae. Eurystheus commanded Heracles to carry out twelve seemingly impossible tasks, or labours.

1. SLAYING THE NEMEAN LION

For his first labour, Heracles was sent to the region of Nemea, near Corinth, where a monstrous lion stalked the countryside. The lion's hide was invulnerable to weapons, so Heracles could not pierce it with his spears or arrows, nor could he injure the beast with his club. Finally, he wrestled the lion to the ground and strangled it. After delivering the corpse as proof of his success, Heracles skinned the lion with one of its own claws and took its impenetrable skin as his armour.

2. SLAYING THE LERNEAN HYDRA

Heracles was then sent to kill the Hydra, a many-headed monster that inhabited a swamp near the city of Lerna. Heracles attacked the monster in its lair, but every time he cut off one of its heads, two more grew in its place. While Heracles was fighting, Hera sent a crab to bite him, but he crushed the crab beneath his foot. He called for help from Iolaus, his nephew, who brought a blazing firebrand. After Heracles cut off each head, Iolaus scorched the stumps to prevent them from growing back. At last the Hydra was defeated, and Heracles dipped his arrows into its poisonous blood, making them lethal.

3. CAPTURING THE CERYNEIAN HIND

Next, Heracles was sent to capture the Hind of Ceryneia. With bronze hooves and golden antlers, this female deer was sacred to Artemis. Heracles pursued the creature all over Greece in a chase that lasted more than a year. Eventually he was able to trap it by pinning its legs together with an arrow. He carried the otherwise unharmed deer back to Mycenae.

4. CAPTURING THE ERYMANTHIAN BOAR

For his fourth task, Heracles had to catch a fierce boar that was ravaging Mount Erymanthus. Despite its size, the boar was very agile and evaded capture. At last, Heracles chased it into a snowdrift, where it became wedged. He hauled it back to Eurystheus, who was so scared that he hid in a large jar until Heracles took the beast away!

5. CLEANING THE AUGEAN STABLES

Then Heracles had to clean out the stables of King Augeas in a single day. Augeas had thousands of cattle, and his stables had not been cleaned for many years. Rather than shovel all the stinking muck by hand, Heracles knocked holes in the stable walls and diverted two rivers so that their water flowed through the shed until it was spotless.

6. DEFEATING THE STYMPHALIAN BIRDS

Next, Heracles had to drive away a flock of man-eating birds from Lake Stymphalus. They attacked people with their metal-tipped feathers and razor-sharp beaks, and they were so numerous that their droppings poisoned the crops. Heracles frightened them into the air with a rattle from Athena. He killed many with his arrows before the rest flew far away.

7. CAPTURING THE CRETAN BULL

Heracles was next sent to the island of Crete to capture a huge bull that was terrorising the population. The bull had been intended as a sacrifice to the gods, but King Minos of Crete could not bring himself to kill it, so instead it was running amok all over the island. Heracles captured the bull and took it back to Eurystheus. Eventually it was released, and it was later killed by the hero Theseus.

8. STEALING THE MARES OF DIOMEDES

Diomedes was an evil king who owned a herd of man-eating mares, which he fed with the flesh of his unfortunate subjects. Heracles rounded up the horses and loaded them aboard his ship. He then defeated Diomedes and his soldiers and fed the king to his own horses. After they had eaten, the mares became quieter and Heracles was able to bridle them and take them to Mycenae.

9. OBTAINING THE GIRDLE OF HIPPOLYTE

King Eurystheus wanted to give his daughter the magic golden belt belonging to Hippolyte, the queen of the Amazons, so he sent Heracles to fetch it. Hippolyte fell in love with Heracles and readily agreed to give him the belt. However, the goddess Hera spread the rumour among the Amazons that Heracles had come to kidnap Hippolyte. The warlike women attacked Heracles, and fearing that Hippolyte had betrayed him, he killed her, then removed the magic girdle from her body and sailed back to Greece.

10. STEALING THE COWS OF GERYON

Heracles was then sent to the far-western Mediterranean to capture a herd of cows that belonged to Geryon, a fierce giant with three heads and six arms. When Heracles arrived, he was attacked by a two-headed dog, Orthus, which he killed with his club. He then killed the giant with some poisoned arrows before taking the cows back to Greece.

11. STEALING THE GOLDEN APPLES OF THE HESPERIDES

Next, Heracles had to collect some golden apples, guarded by the dragon Ladon, from the garden of three nymphs called the Hesperides. In one version of the story, Heracles convinced Atlas—a Titan charged with holding up the heavens—to get the apples for him by offering to take Atlas's place while the Titan fetched the fruit. Atlas readily accepted the bargain but afterwards was loath to take back his heavy burden. So Heracles tricked him by agreeing to stay but asking the Titan to support the weight briefly while the hero went to get a cushion for his shoulders. Heracles then took the apples and returned to Mycenae.

12. CAPTURING CERBERUS

The final labour was the most terrifying of all. Heracles was sent to the underworld to bring back Cerberus, Hades' three-headed dog. Hades treated Heracles with respect because of his strength and skill. The god agreed that he could take the dog on the condition that he subdue the animal with his bare hands. Heracles wrestled Cerberus, squeezing his three throats until he was weak enough to be dragged to the surface. Back at Mycenae, Eurystheus was so scared of Cerberus that, true to form, he hid inside a bronze jar and declared that Heracles was free to go.

> ACTIVITY: Write a list of twelve modern "impossible" labours that you might ask Heracles to perform if you were King Eurystheus today. Think about how you might perform the labours. Use your imagination freely!

LESSON XXI
ATALANTA AND THE CALYDONIAN BOAR

ATALANTA WAS A WILD CHILD. Abandoned by her father, she was raised among the animals of the forest and was protected by the goddess Artemis. She grew up to be a woman as strong as any man, and she could outshoot most of them with her bow and arrows. Atalanta is best known for her part in the hunt for the great boar of Calydon.

THE HUNTING PARTY

Once there was a wild and savage boar causing havoc in the countryside around the Greek city of Calydon. It trampled through fields of ripe grain, tore up orchards and vineyards, and killed dozens of farm animals with its sharp, curved tusks. The boar was such a problem that the city recruited the best hunters in Greece to go out and kill it. Atalanta was included in the group because of her hunting skills, but her presence was resented by most of the male hunters; in ancient Greece, women were expected to stay at home, not to go hunting.

A FATAL OUTCOME

The boar was both quick and cunning, and Atalanta was one of the few hunters to hit it with an arrow, although she only wounded it. Her success made some of the other hunters angry, and they made spiteful remarks about her. Eventually, the hero Meleager succeeded in killing the boar. He paid tribute to Atalanta's skill by offering to share the honour of the kill with her and giving her the boar's skin. The other hunters objected loudly to this, and swords were drawn. Meleager killed two of them, and the others ran away.

THE WEDDING RACE

Her skill and strength made Atalanta very proud, and she announced that she would marry only a man who could beat her in a running race. Many young men tried, but she was always able to defeat them. One young man named Hippomenes, who was desperately in love with Atalanta, begged the goddess Aphrodite for help. She gave him some small golden apples and told him to drop them one at a time during the race. Atalanta kept stopping to pick up the apples, so Hippomenes was able to win the race. It was not, however, to be a long and happy marriage. Atalanta and her new husband disrespected Zeus, and the god punished them both by turning them into lions.

ACTIVITY: Can you find out which god or goddess sent the savage boar to Calydon and why?

LESSON XXII
THE OLYMPIC GAMES

ATHLETIC PROWESS was very highly regarded by the ancient Greeks, and athletic contests or games were a central part of religious life. Some of these contests were small and purely local events, while others were much grander affairs that were open to contestants from all over the Greek-speaking world. The most important of these contests were the Olympic games, first held in 776 BC.

SACRED PEACE

The Olympic games were held every four years near a sacred grove of trees at Olympia, in western Greece. Legend has it that Heracles created the games after completing his twelve labours. They were dedicated to the god Zeus and were intended to promote peace. No fighting was permitted anywhere in Greece while the games were taking place, so wars and other disputes were suspended for their duration. A temple to Zeus, containing a huge statue of the god made by the sculptor Phidias, was built at Olympia.

PRICELESS PRIZES

The first Olympic games had only a single event: a running race called a *stadion* over a distance of a little more than 200 yards. The contestants did not compete for prizes of money or gold but for honour and glory alone: the winner of each event received only a simple crown of olive leaves as a prize. Successful athletes often had statues built of themselves, which they dedicated to the gods, placing them around the temple of Zeus.

LET THE GAMES BEGIN

There were soon many more events added to the games, from chariot racing to wrestling. The *hoplitodromos* was a warriors' race in which competitors ran while wearing a helmet and armour and carrying a shield. The pentathlon combined five separate events: discus throwing, the long jump, javelin throwing, running, and, finally, wrestling.

Throwing the discus requires skill, strength, agility, and balance.

Hoplites (armoured foot soldiers) had their own Olympic event.

OLYMPIC ATHLETES

The ancient Olympic games were staged regularly at Olympia for more than a thousand years, until AD 393. Usually, only male athletes could participate, although some women could own horses and take part in chariot races. There were separate men's and boys' divisions for the events. Athletes had to live apart from their families in a temporary village at Olympia for the duration of the games.

Chariot racing, with teams of specially trained horses, was a very popular event. Sometimes even princes and kings took part.

ACTIVITY: Design your own pentathlon for the Olympic games. Which sports would you include?

LESSON XXIII
ANCIENT GREEK THEATRE

IT IS GENERALLY BELIEVED that the ancient Greeks invented theatre. Like the athletic contests, theatre probably had its origin in acts of religious worship. The first "actors" were most likely priests playing the parts of gods and enacting stories from the myths. In later times, writers started to produce the first plays intended for public entertainment rather than worship.

AESCHYLUS

The playwright Aeschylus lived in Athens around 500 BC. He is the earliest Greek writer whose work has survived to be seen by modern audiences. Aeschylus wrote more than ninety plays, including three tragedies (plays in which the hero comes to a bad end) about King Agamemnon— murdered by his wife, Clytemnestra—and his ill-fated offspring. These three plays are together known as the *Oresteia*, after Agamemnon's son, Orestes, who avenged his father's death by killing his mother and was punished for it by the Furies.

A Fury

SOPHOCLES

Sophocles lived in Athens in the fifth century BC, when the city was at war with Sparta. He is another of the ancient Greek playwrights best known for his tragedies. Sophocles wrote more than a hundred plays, but only seven of them have survived. The most famous are the Theban plays, about the unfortunate hero Oedipus, who unintentionally killed his own father.

Oedipus and the Sphinx

ARISTOPHANES

Not all ancient Greek plays were gloomy tragedies about gods and punishments. Like modern audiences, the Greeks also enjoyed watching comedy. Aristophanes, who was born around 450 BC, was one of the most popular writers of comedies. He sometimes wrote about the gods, but his stories were always humorous. His play *The Birds*, for example, pokes gentle fun at Greek religion through an imaginary visit to the Kingdom of the Birds. In another play, *The Clouds*, his humour is aimed at the citizens of Athens, and he makes jokes about their fashionable manners and clothing.

Greek theatres were open to the skies so that the gods looking down from Olympus could also enjoy the actors' performances.

ACTIVITY: In Sophocles' play *Oedipus Rex*, the Sphinx asks the hero, "What goes on four legs in the morning, two at noon, and three in the evening?" Oedipus hits upon the answer: "Man." The Sphinx is comparing man's life to a day. In the morning of life, when he is a baby, man crawls on his hands and feet (four "legs"). In the middle of life, when he is an adult, he walks on two legs. And in the evening of life, when he is old, he uses a cane (making three "legs"). Can you make up your own riddle to describe a creature or an everyday object?

LESSON XXIV
THE TROJAN WAR

SEVERAL ANCIENT GREEK PLAYS are based on the events of the Trojan War. We know the story of this mythical war in great detail, because the poet Homer wrote much of it down in a book called the *Iliad*. The war takes its name from Troy, a powerful city in what is now Turkey. It began when Paris, a Trojan prince, kidnapped Helen, the wife of Menelaus, who was the Greek king of Sparta.

TEN YEARS OF WAR

With the support of his brother, King Agamemnon of Mycenae, Menelaus gathered an army from all over Greece to journey to Troy and rescue Helen. The Greeks' fleet was said to have numbered a thousand ships, which landed on the coast near Troy. The soldiers pulled their ships up onto the beach and surrounded the towering city walls, which were built of strong stone. The Greeks had no way of breaking down the walls, so they jeered at the Trojans to come out and fight. The Trojans, however, preferred to stand atop the walls and hurl insults and stones at the Greeks. Occasionally one side or the other would make a raid, or several Greek and Trojan warriors would engage in single combat, but no side really gained an advantage, and the war dragged on for ten long years.

ODYSSEUS'S PLAN

At long last, the Greek general Odysseus came up with an ingenious plan. He instructed the Greeks to build a huge, hollow wooden horse as a "gift" for the Trojans. Odysseus hid inside the horse with the best fighters while the rest of the fleet pretended to set sail. The Greek leaders made an elaborate show of packing up their camp, making sacrifices to the gods, and ceremoniously marching their men back aboard their ships.

THE TROJAN HORSE

After watching the Greek ships sail away, the Trojans hauled the mighty wooden horse into their city and began a night of feasting to celebrate their supposed victory. When the Trojans were all asleep, Odysseus and his warriors climbed out of the wooden horse, killed the guards, and let the rest of the Greeks (who had only sailed to a nearby island) into the city. Although they fought bravely, the Trojans stood no chance. They were defeated, and Helen was eventually reunited with her husband, Menelaus.

The Greeks' gift: the horse is left for the Trojans.

ACTIVITY: Imagine that you are one of the Greek commanders. Can you think of another ingenious plan to get your troops into the city of Troy?

LESSON XXV
BELLEROPHON AND PEGASUS

THE WINGED HORSE PEGASUS is one of the most well-known creatures of Greek mythology, but few people know the full story of this famous flying steed that could be ridden by only one man—Bellerophon.

FROM A GORGON'S BLOOD

When the hero Perseus cut off Medusa's snake-haired head, her blood gushed onto the ground. Considering the deadly ugliness of this Gorgon, the spilled blood produced a most unlikely result: Pegasus, a beautiful winged horse. Pegasus was completely wild and stayed far away from humans. Many people tried to ride him, but none of them succeeded—until Bellerophon made the attempt, with a little help from the goddess Athena.

DEATH SENTENCE

Bellerophon was a prince who was descended from the kings of Corinth. His birth name was Hipponous, but he changed it after he fled Corinth, having killed his enemy Belleros (*Bellerophon* means "killer of Belleros"). He sought refuge with King Proetus in the nearby city of Argos, but the king's wife made

spiteful accusations against him. Proetus wanted to kill Bellerophon but didn't dare because he feared the vengeance of the Furies, so he sent him to King Iobates of Lycia with a letter requesting that he be put to death. Iobates also was too afraid of the Furies to kill Bellerophon directly, so he gave him what he thought was an impossible task: to kill the Chimera, the monstrous offspring of Typhon and Echidna.

SLAYING THE CHIMERA

Bellerophon was a skilful fighter, but he could not approach the Chimera on the ground because of the force of its fiery breath. He sought the assistance of the goddess Athena, who gave him a magic bridle that allowed him to harness and tame Pegasus. Mounted on the back of the magnificent flying horse, Bellerophon was able to thrust a lance tipped with lead into the Chimera's terrifying mouth. The monster's fiery breath melted the lead, which scorched the creature's insides and suffocated it. Bellerophon then went on to win battles against the enemies of King Iobates, including the warlike Amazons.

PRIDE BEFORE A FALL

Being able to ride Pegasus made it easy for Bellerophon to perform heroic deeds, so he became very bigheaded. He decided that he was too good to live on Earth and deserved to live with the gods. He commanded Pegasus to fly up to Olympus, and the loyal steed obeyed. Mighty Zeus was outraged by Bellerophon's presumptuous pride, and he sent a gadfly to sting the winged horse as he flew. Pegasus bucked, Bellerophon was thrown off, and the hero fell to Earth, where he wandered, poor and alone, for the rest of his days. As for Pegasus, Zeus later transformed him into a constellation of stars to honour him for his faithful service.

ACTIVITY: The ancient Greeks referred to the extreme pride of Bellerophon as *hubris*, which is what led to his downfall. In other stories, King Agamemnon and the hero Achilles also show *hubris*. Can you find out more about their stories?

APPENDIX I

TIMELINE OF ANCIENT GREEK HISTORY

THE GREEK WRITER HERODOTUS (c. 485–425 BC*) became known as the Father of History because he was the first to record a comprehensive account of real events as opposed to the activities of gods and heroes. Here are some of the key events in ancient Greek history.

c. 900 BC
Greek colonists begin settling on islands and coastlines in the eastern Mediterranean.

c. 800 BC
Greek traders in present-day Syria begin using an alphabet to write down the Greek language. This new means of communication spreads to cities throughout Greece.

776 BC
The first Olympic games are held.

c. 725 BC
Greek colonists settle along the coasts of Sicily and Italy.

c. 620 BC
Greek traders start using coins marked with the symbols of the cities where they were made.

546 BC
Greek cities in modern Turkey are conquered by the Persians.

Ships powered by oars and sails enabled the Greeks to explore the Mediterranean.

499 BC
Greek cities in modern Turkey rebel against Persian rule.

490 BC
The Greeks defeat a Persian invasion at the Battle of Marathon.

480 BC
The Greeks defeat another Persian invasion at sea in the Battle of Salamis.

c. 431–404 BC
The Peloponnesian War is fought by
Athens against the Peloponnesian League, led by Sparta.

Athens was burned during the second Persian invasion but was rebuilt with magnificent temples.

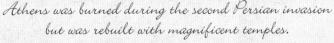

338 BC
King Philip II of Macedon defeats the forces of Athens and Thebes at the Battle of Chaeronea, giving him control over all of Greece.

331 BC
Alexander the Great, Philip of Macedon's son, conquers the Persian Empire.

323 BC
Alexander dies in Babylon, and his empire is divided up between his generals.

215 BC
The Greeks form an alliance with the Carthaginians against Rome.

146 BC
The Romans invade, and Greece becomes part of the Roman Empire.

*c. stands for *circa*, which means "about" or "around." It is often
used in historical texts when only approximate dates are available.

APPENDIX II
FAMILY TREE OF GODS, MONSTERS, AND HEROES

THE GREEK MYTHS can be confusing and sometimes contradictory, but it is possible to draw up a family tree of the most important gods, heroes, and monsters. The left-hand page shows the beings that existed before the time of the gods. The right-hand page shows the relationships between some of the gods and heroes.

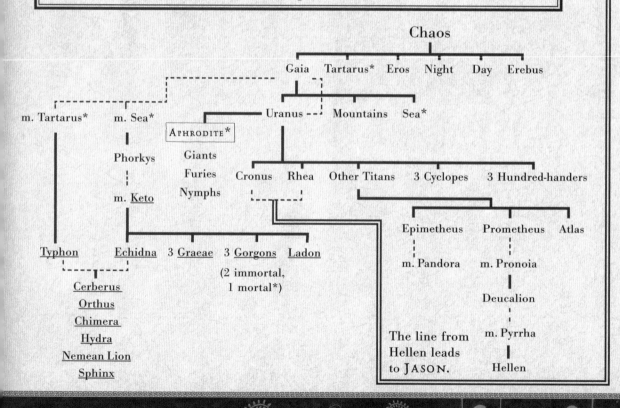

Chaos

Gaia   Tartarus*   Eros   Night   Day   Erebus

Uranus --- Mountains   Sea*

m. Tartarus*   m. Sea*

APHRODITE*

Phorkys   Giants
          Furies   Cronus   Rhea   Other Titans   3 Cyclops   3 Hundred-handers
m. Keto   Nymphs

Epimetheus   Prometheus   Atlas

Typhon   Echidna   3 Graeae   3 Gorgons   Ladon

(2 immortal,
1 mortal*)

m. Pandora   m. Pronoia

Cerberus
Orthus
Chimera   Deucalion
Hydra
Nemean Lion   The line from   m. Pyrrha
Sphinx   Hellen leads
              to JASON.   Hellen

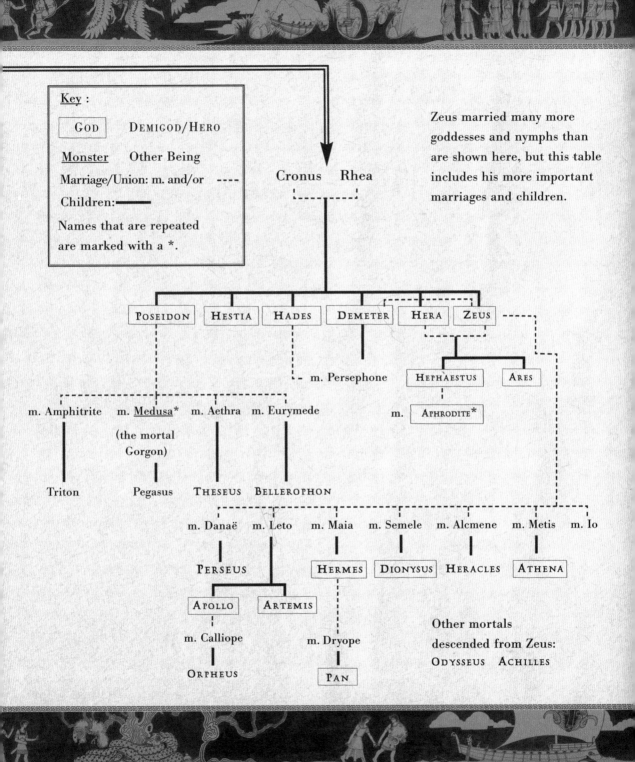

Key :

| GOD | DEMIGOD/HERO |

Monster   Other Being

Marriage/Union: m. and/or   ----

Children:——

Names that are repeated
are marked with a *.

Cronus   Rhea

Zeus married many more
goddesses and nymphs than
are shown here, but this table
includes his more important
marriages and children.

| POSEIDON | HESTIA | HADES | DEMETER | HERA | ZEUS |

m. Persephone

| HEPHAESTUS | ARES |

m. | APHRODITE* |

m. Amphitrite   m. Medusa*   m. Aethra   m. Eurymede

(the mortal
Gorgon)

Triton   Pegasus   THESEUS   BELLEROPHON

m. Danaë   m. Leto   m. Maia   m. Semele   m. Alcmene   m. Metis   m. Io

PERSEUS

| HERMES | | DIONYSUS | | HERACLES | | ATHENA |

| APOLLO | | ARTEMIS |

m. Calliope   m. Dryope

ORPHEUS

| PAN |

Other mortals
descended from Zeus:
ODYSSEUS   ACHILLES

APPENDIX III
GREEKS AND ROMANS

THE ROMANS adopted many aspects of Greek civilisation through contact with Greek cities in Italy and later when they invaded Greece itself. They used a similar system of writing and worshipped many of the Greek gods, although they had different names for these gods.

THE ANCIENT GREEK ALPHABET

Our modern alphabet is based on the Roman alphabet, which in turn was based on the ancient Greek alphabet. The first thing to note about the Greek alphabet is that although some of the letters are familiar, they may not be equivalent to ours. For example, the Greek letter ρ, which looks like our letter *p*, was called *rho* and had the same sound as our letter *r*. There are other differences, too.

For instance, the Greeks had no letters for *j* or *v* and used the Greek equivalents of the letters *i* and *b* for these sounds. Also, the Greeks used a single letter for some sounds for which we use two letters, such as θ (*theta*) for the *th* sound, and ψ (*psi*) for the *ps* sound at the start of words. The chart below shows capital and lowercase Greek letters and their names and equivalent English letters.

Α α	[alpha]	**a**	Ν ν	[nu]	**n**
Β β	[beta]	**b or v**	Ξ ξ	[xi]	**x**
Γ γ	[gamma]	**g**	Ο ο	[omicron]	**o**
Δ δ	[delta]	**d**	Π π	[pi]	**p**
Ε ε	[epsilon]	**e**	Ρ ρ	[rho]	**r**
Ζ ζ	[zeta]	**z**	Σ σ	[sigma]	**s**
Η η	[eta]	**e or h**	Τ τ	[tau]	**t**
Θ θ	[theta]	**th**	Υ υ	[upsilon]	**u or y**
Ι ι	[iota]	**i or j**	Φ φ	[phi]	**ph or f**
Κ κ	[kappa]	**c, k, or q**	Χ χ	[chi]	**ch**
Λ λ	[lambda]	**l**	Ψ ψ	[psi]	**ps**
Μ μ	[mu]	**m**	Ω ω	[omega]	**aw or w**

NAMES OF THE GODS AND GODDESSES

Studying the Greek alphabet will allow you to "translate" the Greek names of any gods, heroes, or monsters that you may encounter. The names of the main gods are shown in Greek in the central column below. The names by which the Romans knew them are shown in the right-hand column. Take particular note that the Greek letters ε (*epsilon*) and η (*eta*) were both used to represent slightly different *e* sounds. You may be able to recognise some of the Greek gods' names below, but do not expect them to be exactly the same as they are in English. For example, *Apollo* is usually written ΑΠΟΛΛΩΝ in capital letters and Ἀπόλλων in lowercase letters, which you could translate as *Apollawn* or *Apollon*.

GOD/GODDESS	GREEK NAME	ROMAN NAME
Aphrodite	ΑΦΡΟΔΙΤΗ	Venus
Apollo	ΑΠΟΛΛΩΝ	Apollo
Ares	ΑΡΗΣ	Mars
Artemis	ΑΡΤΕΜΙΣ	Diana
Athena	ΑΘΗΝΑ	Minerva
Demeter	ΔΗΜΗΤΗΡ	Ceres
Dionysus	ΔΙΟΝΥΣΟΣ	Bacchus
Hades	ΑΔΗΣ	Pluto
Hephaestus	ΗΦΑΙΣΤΟΣ	Vulcan
Hera	ΗΡΑ	Juno
Hermes	ΕΡΜΗΣ	Mercury
Hestia	ΕΣΤΙΑ	Vesta
Pan	ΠΑΝ	Silvanus
Poseidon	ΠΟΣΕΙΔΩΝ	Neptune
Zeus	ΖΕΥΣ	Jupiter

ATHENA

ZEUS

Athena, Goddess of Wisdom

Zeus, King of the Gods

HEPHAESTUS

THRA

MACEDONIA

ITALY

APULIA

EPIRUS

Mt. Olympus

Thessaloniki

Mt. Ossa

River Enipeus

CORCYRA

Dodona

Mt. Pelion

Iolcus

Croton

THE IONIAN SEA

Ephyra

THESSALY

Hephaestus, God of Fire

River Acheron

Actium

Straits of Messina

LEVKAS

AITOLIA

PHOCIS

Calydon

Mt. Parnassus

BOEOTIA

SICILY

ITHACA

Delphi

ATTICA

ARTEMIS

Mt. Etna

River Acheloös

Thespiae

Eleus

Syracuse

ZAKYNTHOS

ACHAJA

Gulf of Corinth

Ath

Missolonghi

Nemea

Corinth

Sou

Olympia

Mycenae

MALTA

Mt. Lycaon

Seronic Gulf

ARCADIA

Artemis, Goddess of the Hunt

Sparta

KITHIRA

THE MEDITERRANEAN SEA

Mt. Ida

Map
OF
ANCIENT
Greece

DIONYSUS

Poseidon, God of the Sea

Dionysus, God of Wine

POSEIDON

HERA

ARES

Hera, Queen of the Gods

Ares, God of War

BLACK SEA

Stamboul

PROPONTIS

APHRODITE

Aphrodite, Goddess of Love

OTHRACE
NOS
Hellespont   Troy   MYSIA
TENEDOS   Mt. Ida

PHRYGIA

LESBOS
THE
GEAN SEA

LYDIA

CHIOS

Smyrna

Key

CITIES   TEMPLES
MOUNTAINS   ORACLES
CAVES

Ephesus

CARIA

DELOS
THE CYCLADES

Halicarnassus

Apollo, God of Music

NAXOS

SANTORINI

Heraklion

RHODES   Lindos

APOLLO

Knossos

Dicte
RETE

DEMETER

HERMES

Demeter, Goddess of the Harvest

Hermes, Messenger of the Gods

Cartography
BY
E. Nicholls
The Twelve Olympians
courtesy of
N. Palin

SOLUTIONS

LESSON I (p. 13)

1. B   2. E   3. D   4. A   5. C

LESSON II (p. 15)

1. Urania   3. Euterpe
2. Melpomene   4. Thalia

LESSON V (p. 21)

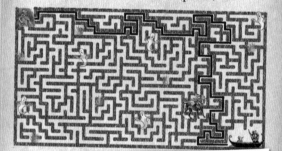

LESSON XIII (p. 41)

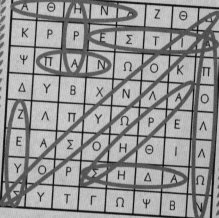

The gods and goddesses shown in Greek in the word search are:
Athena (ΑΘΗΝΑ), Hera (ΗΡΑ), Hestia (ΕΣΤΙΑ), Pan (ΠΑΝ), Zeus (ΖΕΥΣ), Dionysus (ΔΙΟΝΥΣΟΣ), Ares (ΑΡΗΣ), Hades (ΑΔΗΣ), and Apollo (ΑΠΟΛΛΩΝ).

LESSON XV (p. 45)

PUBLISHER'S NOTE

The original volume of *The Mythology Handbook* contained a set of colourful gummed images at the back, presumably intended by Lady Hestia to be an amusing learning aid for her children. Clearly, her intent was to present the wonders of Greek mythology in an entertaining manner. We have faithfully reproduced the images here in the form of stickers, which we hope will provide similar amusement for the modern mythologist.

LESSON XIX (p. 57)

1. D   2. C   3. B   4. A